A First Flight® Level Two Reader

NO FROGS
for
DINNER

by Frieda Wishinsky

Illustrated by Linda Hendry

Fitzhenry & Whiteside • Toronto

First published in the United States in 1999.

Fitzhenry & Whiteside acknowledges with thanks the support of the
Government of Canada through its Book Publishing Industry Development
Program in the publication of this title.

Printed in Hong Kong.
Cover and book design by Wycliffe Smith Design.

10 9 8 7 6 5 4 3 2 1

Canadian Cataloguing in Publication Data

Wishinsky, Frieda
No frogs for dinner
(A first flight level two reader)
"First flight books"

ISBN 1-55041-519-0 (bound)
ISBN 1-55041-521-2 (pbk.)

I.Hendry, Linda.   II. Series: First flight reader.

PS8595.I834N6 1999   jC813'.54   C99-931308-8
PZ7.W78032No 1999

For my friend,
Kathy Guttman

F.W.

———————

For Chris and Janet
Who only make "good" things to eat...

L.H.

Melvin couldn't wait to visit
the big city.

He'd ride up
the tallest
buildings.

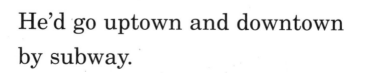

He'd go uptown and downtown
by subway.

He'd watch baseball in a giant stadium.

He'd munch pizza and hot dogs and pretzels.

It would be great!

Finally the day came.

Melvin's parents drove him
to the airport.

"Be a good guest," they said.
"Listen to Aunt Rose."

"I will," Melvin promised.

The plane rose in the sky.

Soon Melvin saw
fluffy clouds.

Soon Melvin saw long bridges.

Soon Melvin saw the city!

With a bounce the plane landed
and Melvin stepped out.

"Melvin! Melvin!"
called Aunt Rose.

She scooped him
into her arms.

She squeezed him
like a tomato.

"Hurry!" she said. "I've planned
EVERYTHING!"

"Everything?" said Melvin,
as they leaped into a cab.

"First the Museum of Natural
History!" said Aunt Rose.

They headed for the
dinosaurs immediately.

Aunt Rose asked Melvin
what the Tyrannosaurus ate.

She asked him
what the Stegosaurus
drank.

She asked him how tall,
how fat, how long, how fast
the Brontosaurus was.

But Melvin couldn't answer.
Aunt Rose answered for him.

15

"Now for the Museum
of Modern Art," said Aunt Rose.

Aunt Rose zipped him
past strange paintings
and sculptures.

She talked about artists,
colors and shapes.

She talked

and talked

and talked.

Finally she stopped talking
and whisked him into a cab.

The cab zigzagged
and zoomed.

"Where are we going?"
asked Melvin.

"Shopping!"
sang Aunt Rose.

"Shopping?"
groaned Melvin.

"First a tie for your dad,"
said Aunt Rose.

"Dad hates ties,"
said Melvin.

"He'll love this one," said
Aunt Rose.

"Now a scarf for your mom,"
said Aunt Rose.

"Mom doesn't
wear scarves,"
said Melvin.

"She'll wear this one!"
said Aunt Rose.

"Now for you!"

"I don't want anything,"
said Melvin.

"Pish posh,"
said Aunt
Rose.

Aunt Rose
picked out a
tee shirt for
Melvin.

"Try it on!" said Aunt Rose.

"I'd rather not,"
said Melvin.

"For me," said Aunt Rose.

Melvin tried on the tee shirt.
Aunt Rose pinched
his cheek.

"You look
adorable.
We'll buy
two!

Now for sushi."

"What's sushi?"
asked Melvin.

"Raw fish wrapped
in fish skins and seaweed."

Melvin ate two bowls of rice.

"Time for the opera!"
sang Aunt Rose.

"I'm a little tired,"
said Melvin.

"The opera will perk you up,"
said Aunt Rose.

At the opera,
the singers
sang

and sang

and sang.

By Act Two Melvin was
sound asleep.

"Poor darling," said Aunt Rose
on the way home.

"Right to bed.
Tomorrow is a
busy day."

Aunt Rose woke him at seven.

She made oatmeal,
stewed prunes
and tea.

"How about a nice poached egg?"
she suggested.

"I'm stuffed,"
said Melvin.

"Don't worry," said Aunt Rose.
"You'll walk it off at the Botanical
Gardens."

Aunt Rose dragged him from
flower to flower.

"Smell this," she said.
"Smell that."

Melvin smelled hundreds of flowers.

"Now, oysters for lunch!"
announced Aunt Rose.

"How do you eat oysters?"
asked Melvin.

"You open your mouth and they
slide down," said Aunt Rose.

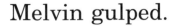

Melvin gulped.

"Aunt Rose," he began, "I...I..."

"You want to know about dinner. We're having frogs' legs."

"What?"
Melvin gasped.

"Frogs, darling, frogs!"
sang Aunt Rose.

Melvin stared at Aunt Rose.

He couldn't.
He wouldn't.

"No," he said.

"What?" gasped Aunt Rose.

"NO. I'm not eating frogs," Melvin said.

"No, I'm not eating oysters...

Can we do things I want Aunt Rose?"

Aunt Rose stared at Melvin.

"Why, Melvin, darling,
why didn't you tell me?
You should always speak up."

"I am," said Melvin.

"I want to ride up the
tallest skyscraper.

I want to go uptown
and downtown
by subway.

I want to watch baseball
in a giant stadium.

I want..."

"Stop, Melvin!" said Aunt Rose.
"My head is spinning."

"But can we? Can we?"
asked Melvin.

"Of course we can, darling,"
said Aunt Rose.

"After all, Melvin, you're my guest!"

And Melvin was!